SIRIUS

Science Fiction

Volume 2   2025

Neil Williams (ed.)

Ddyn Books

SIRIUS Science Fiction, Volume 2 2025

Library and Archives Canada Cataloguing in Publication

Williams, Neil, 1958-

    Volume 2 2025-- / Neil Williams.

(SIRIUS Science Fiction)

ISBN 978-1-894602-06-8   I. Title. II. Series: Williams, Neil, 1958- .

SIRIUS Science Fiction.

For more information:
Published by Ddyn Books
an imprint of Uldune Media
504 – 635 Canterbury Street
Woodstock, ON, Canada, L4S 8X9.
info@uldunemedia.ca
https://www.uldunemedia.ca/ddyn.htm

cover art by openart.ai

CONTENTS

EDITORIAL

Being age 16 can be a wonderful time. You are no longer always treated as a child. You do not yet have adult responsibilities. Your life is spread wide open before you. You are young with hormones surging. You and your crowd know everything. Kids are stupid. Adults are stupid. But, you and your friends are wise and brilliant. It is a wonderful time to be so certain, so full of yourself, and so very idiotic.

Looking back at SIRIUS Science Fiction from 1975, I can definitely see the sixteen year old me. I can also observe the binary nature of my worldviews back then. AZ is great always and XB is always bad; it is one or the other. There is no in between, no hues of colour, no shades of grey. I can also see elements that are the precursors to SWILL.

Way back in 1975, I was young and very provincial. I lived in the 'burbs. My exposure to "science fiction fanzines" had not been non-fiction fanzines, but only Star Trek fanfic fanzines. I was going to do produce a fanzine that had original fiction, not Trek fanfic. And so I did. And I published my friends' stories that had previously been published in our high school science fiction magazine. I am not certain what the adults actually thought of SIRIUS #1 other than quaint and provincial; those naive kids out in far Brampton and Georgetown beyond the civilising influences of "Imperial Toronto"...

There was a much shorter #2 issue that was printed on ditto using the high school equipment in October of 1975. It had a single story within it. The editorial stated that this was the final issue and that the magazine would be revived in 1976 as SIRIUS b. Well, that didn't happen.

And that outcome was probably for the best.

So why now?

Because, it has been 50 years. So why not...

I know that there are some digital copies of SIRIUS #1 and #2 out there, on the internet. That is because I scanned them from my aging copies of the two physical issues and emailed them to sf fandom historians. To be bluntly honest, they are rubbish. I have a little nostalgia regarding the two issues as they are my first (albeit horrid) attempts at publication, but that is all. Just a malenky smidgen of nostalgia.

The rationale for this revival is that there are few Canadian markets for science fiction. And in this new age of trade war with the USA and threats of a potential military invasion of Canada by the USA; it is time for a new Canadian market.

My original plan for **SIRIUS Science Fiction Volume 2: 2025** was solicit stories from known Canadian authors at a rate I could currently afford, the same word rate as On Spec, $.05 CAD per word. I had zero takers. Of course, I probably screwed that up by stating that **SIRIUS Science Fiction Volume 3: 2026** would pay current SFWA rates of 0.08 USD per word. It was my intention to only have a single story in this volume. Now, I have three.

And so, there is a clean break from the past. SIRIUS Science Fiction has been reincarnated as a Canadian science fiction market, an annual anthology magazine. This first volume of the new iteration will set the stage, and also be very different. I will initiate the crowdfunding for Volume 3 in March of 2026, at which time the volume theme will be announced. Yes, each volume going forward will have a theme.

Thus, without any further ado...

Neil Williams

Bwana

by Neil Williams

One upon a time I owned and operated a metaphysical shop. The earlier version of this story was much longer and had more character development. The common critique of the story was that it was cute, but too long. They suggested that I set it in the USA and make it shorter. It still didn't sell. I have returned it to a Canadian setting and have decided to publish this final version here...

The aliens arrived on Crazy Santeria Day.

In my business -- I run a small metaphysical supply shop -- every Wednesday is Crazy Santeria Day. We get most of our Santeria clientele two days a week, Fridays and Wednesdays. Friday is 'Steady Santeria Day' where we get a quiet, fairly constant flow of Santeria business. The customers come in with their "prescriptions" to be filled for spellwork, and some may get a reading, but most of the traffic arrives with a list in-hand, either on paper or on their mobile device. It is a good day, business-wise, without the drama.

Wednesdays, though, are different. The traffic comes in waves and the Santeria customers exhibit a high level of paranoia and intensity. Everybody needs an immediate reading, plus the magical protection, counter-measures, or payback to combat the hexes that they know have been cast upon them. Naturally, Wednesday is the best sales day of the week -- it is also the most chaotic.

This particular Wednesday began no differently than most. John Wellington Wells Limited, my shop, is a small storefront establishment on the ground floor of an eight story apartment building in downtown Dundas. The store is more deep than it is wide and at 10:30 AM it was already crowded, and noisy and the business brisk. I was at the counter making up spellwork "prescriptions", as well as running the till. Both Gayle (my girlfriend) and Lady Cassie (the part-time reader that I bring in on Wednesdays) were at the back of the store in the Reading Rooms. Matt, my regular part-timer, was engaged in his duties as general fetch and dogsbody. There was an aura of tension and anxiety that permeated the store -- just a typical Wednesday.

A loud static hiss emitted from the store stereo system -- an ancient iPod connected to an all-in-one speaker system. I reached behind me to turn it off when I realized that it was already off. On Wednesdays I never turn it on; the shop is too noisy to begin with. I turned the unit off-and-on, but the static only grew in volume, before it morphed into a clear, relaxed voice. "Greetings to the Human species from the Co-operative of Sentient Beings. We, the Tutumei species, have been assigned the duty of making First Contact with you. You are not alone. That is all."

"What the..." Matt said. There were other voices raised in question and confusion as my customers were pulled from their current troubles to wonder what was going on.

The voice returned, "Your species has a strong potential of actually emerging as a civilization in the not too distant future. First Contact is a simple, 'hello, guess what, you're not alone, see you later when you finish growing up,' and that's it."

Gayle pulled the curtain back from her Reading Room and gave me a 'what's this about' look and I raised my arms in a full 'no idea' shrug.

The voice returned, "Should your planetary civilization survive and mature, we will be back -- and yes, it will be the Tutumei who return -- to initiate Second Contact. See you on our return. Good bye and good luck." The voice paused. "And just to inform you, there will be some of our researchers arriving for a short duration on your planet. There is nothing that you can do to stop this, nor is it possible to capture one of the researchers, nor is it possible to kill one of the researchers. The researchers shall be arriving -- now."

And there was static and then only the murmur of human voices remained.

This was followed by screams, shouts of alarm, and general chaos. While angry, anxiety fuelled screams and shouts are not uncommon on Crazy Santeria Day, wild hysterical screaming and mad stampedes from the shop are. Lady Cassie nearly ripped the curtain off of her Reading Room in her haste to flee the store. In the back left corner, beside the bulletin board and the rack of Alanna Riga spell books, calm and apparently unmoved by all the brouhaha, stood the alien.

The alien was short, maybe 140 centimeters tall, and stocky. It was also humanoid; bipedal, with two arms, a torso, one head on top. The arms were both thicker and shorter than is the norm in humans and ended in hands with four digits, two fingers and two opposable thumbs. Its legs were much more muscular, with feet more like that of a hippo than a human. And that is all there was to describe. The protective suit loosely covered the alien's body except for what appeared to be the alien's head which was enclosed in a spherical helmet. The entire suit was seamless, blacker than jet, with a slight sheen to the material.

As this was my store and somebody had to do something, I stepped out from behind the counter and walked toward the alien. Matt watched me nervously and Gayle shot me a 'be careful' glare. I nodded back to her as I approached the alien. I stopped about half a meter from it and slowly offered my right hand. "Welcome to Earth," I began and then stumbled into new customer mode. "I am the owner of this establishment, Dylan Jones. How can I help you?"

The alien daintily took my hand, as if it were afraid that it would accidentally crush it, and we shook briefly. The suit as cool to the touch and slidey; not slippery -- it wasn't wet – but more like not even dust would adhere to it. Matt latter called it frictionless.

"Thank you for your greeting Mr. Jones," the alien said. The alien's voice was the same as in the broadcast message, probably the same translation program, or something like that. "My personal names do not translate well. As there is a gap our respective techno-cultural levels, and your species is most certainly benightedly provincial and verging on the primitive, I have selected a Human name you may use. You may call me, Bwana."

"Okay, Bwana." I was ticked off about the primitive comment, but decided to just leave it. I gestured to Gayle and Matt. "This is Gayle Davidson and Matt Pentland; they both work in the shop with me."

"Greetings Ms Davidson, Mr. Pentland. Ms Davidson, would you be Mr. Jones mate or..."

"Something like that," she responded, with a smile. "Dylan and I live together."

"Mr. Jones, as the owner of this establishment, would I be correct in the assumption that you could close the store for about an hour while we talked?"

I laughed. "I think that we can manage that."

"You kind of chased all the business away," Matt added. Gayle shot him a look. "Umm, sorry. I didn't mean to blame..."

No offence taken, Mr. Pentland." Bwana indicated the chairs over in the Reading area. "Shall we, Mr. Jones?" Bwana walked past me toward them and I followed. The floorboards visibly gave under Bwana's weight, he may be short but he is heavy.

"Matt, could you put up the 'Closed' sign and lock the door?"

"Sure." He walked behind the counter to get the keys.

Close the blinds too," I said to him as I walked over to Gayle's reading table.

Gayle had already taken her seat behind the table. I picked up one of the overturned chairs, righted it and sat down. Bwana didn't sit, though he appeared to have relaxed his weight; the floor warped slightly under where he stood.

"So, what do you want to talk about?" I asked.

"Dylan, how do you think the Co-operative operates?"

Matt came over with a chair and his sketchpad. "Would it be okay if I..."

"Drew me?" finished Bwana. "Certainly."

Gayle looked at Matt as if he was an idiot, "Why don't you use your phone?"

"All I get is a distorted blur, an unresolved outline..."

"My protective suit disrupts your electronic recordings," Bwana said. "Dylan, my question?"

I shrugged. "I don't know. Some sort of interstellar federation or union, they have some form of First Contact criteria, beyond that – I don't know. Maybe when a species is close to meeting the membership requirements, that is when the Co-operative makes contact"

"I disagree." said Matt. "I think it is more a matter of space being really big. Different spacefaring aliens make contact with each other when and if they run into each other."

"Agreed," Bwana replied. "Though to some extent Dylan is also correct, there are contact criteria."

Gayle played with the dangly part of her right earring. "So, if First Contact is just a simple 'hi, bye, catch you later'. What happens with Second Contact?"

"That I cannot tell you," Bwana said. "What do you think happens?"

"With our Co-op membership, we get access to an interstellar drive," Matt blurted.

"No! An encyclopedia galactica and connection to an interstellar internet," stated Gayle.

"I don't think so," I said. "Both are too much. Probably just some form of trade deal and an embassy."

Matt laughed. "Such a capitalist, they probably don't even have money..."

"Or maybe they do." I looked at Bwana. "Do you?"

"I cannot say."

"Bwana, I would think that an interstellar civilization would have a post-scarcity economy, wouldn't they?" Gayle raised an eyebrow. "Interstellar travel must be expensive."

"Do you think so?" Bwana asked.

"I would." I leaned forward. "I have a feeling that you have some form of Faster-Than-Light travel, but not as simple as in our science fiction shows. There must be some limitations on the star drive -- range, speed, energy use. Otherwise, aliens would be showing up every other month."

"Maybe they will, starting now," said Gayle. "Someone has to be the first."

"No," said Matt. "I am certain that the Co-op only has sub-light space drive. That is why Bwana's people have been assigned to us; they are nearby -- within 100 light-years."

"That's still pretty far," I replied.

Gayle nodded. "Way too far. And how would they run the Co-op if there wasn't at least something like Faster-Than-Light communication. I still think they would have warp drive.

I raised an eyebrow. "Maybe, but I still think their drive has restrictions. But they would need hyperspace or warp drive to have any form of interstellar state..."

"Or the whole government is run by AIs," offered Matt. "The distances and time lags would mean nothing to machine intelligences. Everything could operate at sub-light or at light speed."

Bwana began to make a hissing noise which startled all three of us. This continued for thirty seconds before it began to lower in volume, but it didn't stop.

Gayle moved her hand across the table toward the alien. "Bwana, are you alright?"

"I think he's fine," said Matt. "You're laughing at us, aren't you, Bwana?""

The hissing ceased. "I am, Matt. Oh yes, I really am." There was a single brief hiss. "This is absolutely priceless! You just can't write this stuff and have it seem at all plausible. Only out of the mouths of primitives, who actually believe in the rubbish they are spouting, do the true gems emerge. The audience back home is going to love this material..."

"Audience? Material? Your people said that you were a researcher," said Matt, "but you're talking like a TV producer."

And I am, both," said Bwana. "But, we Tutumei do have some similarities with Humans. We have a sense of humor and we also have entertainment media. I am a researcher involved in content acquisition for one of our more popular programs"

"Interstellar Wild Kingdom?" Gayle was not at all amused, but Bwana seemed to be oblivious, or unconcerned, or both.

"No, not at all; you are sentients. This program is similar to a political satire show from France that was completely devoted to segments like this."

"So," I said, "If I understand you correctly, we're going to appear on one of your comedy shows..."

"As objects of ridicule, no less," Gayle added.

Matt finished drawing and set down his charcoal on the table. "What's the show called?"

Bwana said nothing. "This is difficult to translate, figuratively -- it involves a play on words in our major language and cultural context. A literal translation would be, 'Residents of Uncivilized Worlds are Cretinous Nincompoops'."

"Sort of like, 'Talking to Barbarians'," said Matt.

"Exactly," said Bwana.

"Well, that fits what I've drawn here." Matt held up the sketchpad for all of us to see.

It was a caricature; that's what Matt does when he isn't working for me. There was Bwana in the black shiny environmental suit, next to Gayle, Matt, and I. We were all some sort of cavepeople, dressed in hides. I held a large wooden staff and my hair all slicked back with woad. Gayle wasn't wearing very much, just a hide one-piece swimdress and bodypaint; she was doing some spellwork -- judging by the stars and swirls she was calling forth between her hands. Matt was our porter, loaded down with a variety of metaphysical supplies -- all made of wood and stone and leather -- sticking out of a hide backpack-like contraption.

"May I keep this?" Bwana asked.

Matt shrugged. "Sure." He passed the sketchpad to Bwana.

"Wait a minute," said Gayle. "I'm not certain I want that depiction of me," she flashed Matt a look, "going up all over your alien internet."

"That won't happen. This is more of what you would call..." He paused and then stood fully erect. The floorboards relaxed slightly. "I think that my time here is up."

There was the smash of broken glass followed by tear gas. With a dull thud and more broken glass, the shop door was forced open. In rushed a Tactical Unit of the Hamilton Police Services, along with some guys in black suits (probably CSIS), all shouting at us to stay where we were. I was coughing and my vision was blurring from the gas, but I could still make out Bwana standing beside me. He stood there still unmoving, and then he was gone.

The authorities took all three of us away, to separate locations. I was sufficiently questioned, harangued, and intimidated. As part of the interrogation process, CSIS did threaten to hand me over to Homeland Security in the USA. For the moment it did seem that I was destined for a one-way transport to Guantanamo and the pleasures of enhanced interrogation.

Fortunately, the Tutumei took over all of Earth's communications mediums for one final broadcast. They cautioned humankind's leaderships, in a school principal manner, that continued incarceration, torture, and murder of those humans who had interacted with the Tutumei researchers was being documented and recorded. This behaviour could result in a reclassification of the Human species.

We were all released five days later.

The shop was a wreck. The cops and the spooks had deployed too many tear gas bombs and one of them started a fire in the back of the store where I made up many of the metaphysical oils. My store, and the pet supply shop next door, were burnt out shells. Gayle and I surveyed the damage to see if there was anything worth salvaging; there wasn't.

As soon as we were released and reunited; I proposed to Gayle. This time she said, yes. The insurance money for the shop was much more than it should have been, I contacted the company and they assured me that the sum was correct. Gayle received a significant inheritance from a relative she never even heard of. Matt was accepted into the Ontario College of Art on full scholarship; he also received a substantial commission to create a mural for the head office of one of the major chartered banks. Gayle and I purchased a condo apartment together in Dundas.

When we moved into our condo, there were two things waiting for us. A painting in the living room and on the kitchen counter about a ream of white 8 1/2 by 11 paper with a card stock cover fastened by brass brads. There was a note attached to the cover.

> Dylan, Gayle, and Matt,
> Thank you for spending time with me.
> Matt, the Tutumei are not as distantly advanced as you think we are. I believe that this picture more accurately depicts the techno-cultural gap between our two species.
> Dylan and Gayle, this is the "series bible" for a comedy-drama I have written. Nobody has "picked it up" on my world. Perhaps "Left Behind Among the Sloth-

Brained Savages" may find a home with you Humans. Consider this a wedding present.

May you all have a happy life and good luck,
Bwana

The painting was a caricature in color that mimicked Matt's style. Bwana stood in the centre wearing his black environmental suit. Matt stood next to Bwana on the left and I stood on Bwana's right side, with Gayle standing beside me to my left. Bwana had each arm resting, gingerly, on both my shoulder and Matt's, and I had my left arm around Gayle's waist. All three humans had cheesy advertising smiles on our faces and maybe Bwana did too. All three humans were dressed in Victorian era clothing. Matt was holding a wire that ran to some automated clockwork contraption connected to a nineteenth century camera that was taking the picture.

We gave Matt the original painting from Bwana; a few months later he gave us a reproduction that he had painted. It hangs in the family room of the home that Gayle and I now share with our two children. "Abandoned on Earth" has won four Canadian Screen awards and one Emmy -- the sixth season premiers this fall.

Print Medium Review:

The Downloaded (2024)

Robert J. Sawyer
ISBN 978-1-989398-99-9

I have always enjoyed the works of Robert J. Sawyer and he is one
science fiction author which both my wife and I like. The Downloaded
hits on a lot of Sawyer's themes and began its life as a concept for a CGI
animated series back in 1999 and went through a series of iterations (you
can read Sawyer's tale here https://sfwriter.com/dlorigin.htm) until it
reached the final one as an audiobook released in 2023 and a trade
paperback published in 2024.

This is a review of the print book.

The major themes that Sawyer uses are uploaded/downloaded
consciousness, quantum computing, AI and robotics, transhumanism, and
interstellar flight. The central theme revolves around uploaded
consciousness and quantum computing. Using the theory that human
consciousness is due to our brains engaging in quantum level processing
and that the only appropiate upload would be a quantum computer, which
would maintain the entanglement of the consciousness in its storage.
That cryogenics will not work until you have a sufficient quantum
computer to upload a human consiousness into, and then into the revived
body.

The setting is 2059 in Waterloo, Ontario. Two groups of people have
been uploaded into the the quantum computer, a crew of astronauts who
will crew humankind's first interstellar voyage and a pilot programme for
prisoners (the prisoners serve their time in virtual reality at a higher clock
rate so a 20 years sentance served is only 18 months in real time). We
hear that there is a Mars colony, and orbital space tourism, and problems
on Earth (of course, there are always problems on Earth...)

The prime officers of the interstellar crew are the first to be awakened after their 500 year interstellar voyage. But, there is a problem. They are still on Earth. The starship is still in orbit and never left the Solar System. And civilisation has collapsed. And when the prisoners are awakened, the problems increase. In addition there is a neighbouring Menonite community, and someone unknown observing the research institute in what was Waterloo, Ontario in Canada.

I will not give spoilers...

There is discussion of what are the rights of a sentient robot, and where the 3 Laws of Asimov fail. On whether or not Homo sapiens is fit to leave the confines of Earth. Is it possible to rehabilitate or are criminals are just born bad people; or are just some criminals genetically born criminals. And what does it mean to be human?

The ideas are compelling, the majority of the characters are interesting, and the story (or stories) satisfactory. It definitely IS a Robert Sawyer novel. Is it a great novel? Of that, I am uncertain. I have a feeling that the audio book, which appears to contain elements of an audio drama not just a straight reading of the print book, may actually be superior to the print medium. Nevertheless, it is a good novel and I recommend it.

Neil Williams

The Day the Canadians Came

by Neil Williams

It is somewhat fitting that this story follows a review of a book by Robert Sawyer. Sawyer does not like the Canadian forms of "magical realism", especially the concept of ghosts in space. This story has also done "the rounds" and has been criticised for the "ghosts in space" concept, and for being too Canadian. This is the first story in a series of stories set in the same universe; that universe is part of a larger universe wherein my far future Greater Community of Worlds stories (e.g., "Learning Curve") are set.

The tenth anniversary is fast approaching and I will be in geosynchronous orbit when that date arrives. So, my bosses in Administration and the Social Media Relations people want me to make a record of my recollections of that event. I have tried to tell them that I was extensively interviewed back in 2041, but they want my own feelings and thoughts as an adult. So here it comes, a monologue.

Grant tells me not to be boring.

Grant Edmundsen was, or is, my best friend. He is now forever, age eight. He is about 127 cm tall, with light brown hair (in a bowl-cut), and grey-green eyes. He doesn't age. No ghosts age. And, as my best friend, Grant follows me everywhere.

I am not a ghost whisperer, a person who coaxes or guides spirits of the departed to enter into the Beyond, the Afterlife, or whatever you want to call it. For the vast majority of people, when they die, their spirit slips easily into the Beyond. Only those souls that believe that they have "unfinished business", actual or imagined, remain. And those ghosts need to be gently prodded or shown the path into the Beyond.

But, if you die in space, especially from Middle Earth Orbit and out, you cannot enter into the Beyond yourself. We do not know why yet. This has only recently become a subject of scientific and empirical study.

It was the Singapore Station Massacre in 2046 that changed everything. An accident occurred, in which 127 people died; then the ghosts of those who had perished, killed every other person on the station. This was all recorded on the security cameras, persons murdered by invisible forces. Documented and analysed. And so, new controls were created.

People like me are part of those controls. Ghost drovers are "ghost bouncers". Metaphysically, we grab the ghost, open a portal into the Beyond, toss the ghost through the portal, and then close it. We don't know a lot yet in this field, but this we do know; ghosts are real. Some people can see ghosts. A small number of those people who can perceive ghosts are also able to manipulate ghosts. I am one of those people. And I am a Mission Specialist with the Canadian Space Agency.

Grant says I have to tell my story. He says that they will show this on a big holo in St. Mary's Park by the Gazebo. And I tell Grant that the Gazebo and park were destroyed by the tanks of the Little Egypt Righteousness Army back in '32. Grant says that the town has rebuilt the park and the Gazebo, better than it was.

I was born in 2025, in Cairo Illinois. And should my hometown come up in conversation, I still correctly call it 'CARE-oh'; instead of the Canadian pronunciation of 'KYE-row'. I don't recall much from the time before, when there was the United States of America.

I guess I started noticing how things were falling apart when I was around age five. The electricity was no longer a constant. It would be on for weeks and then off for days. Then those days became weeks, eventually months. Everyone had a gas generator for the fridge and freezer. Cooking was done on the barbeque. Solar power panels collected electricity to charge the portable power station, so that we could watch TV and charge phones. But the mobile phones could find a network less and less. Dad wasn't working anymore. My parents argued more. But, that was the same for many of my friends too. There was rationing at the supermarket. My favorite cereal, Froot Loops was no longer available. Things were getting worse. But the adults just called it the "new normal" and so we didn't worry. But even if we did worry, there was nothing, as kids, we could do about it."

Grant says I am wrong. Grant was worried. He didn't believe that this was a "new normal". He knew that it would be an "end of everything". It wasn't, the end of everything. It would be, unfortunately, the end of Grant. And the end of many others too.

I don't know why I can see ghosts. I do know when this talent first emerged. That was the day that I saw my Uncle Mike die in October of 2031. I was almost age six when he died. Cairo had been occupied by the Illinois Apostolic Crusade. This was the first army to occupy Cairo during The Chaos. It wouldn't be the last. We were under strict curfew, but the town, newly occupied, did not know how strict. Mom didn't allow smoking in the house, or on the front porch, so Uncle Mike had gone out onto the front lawn to smoke a cigarette.

Then a military patrol turned the corner onto our street. As they passed our home, they opened fire on Uncle Mike. There was blood and he crumpled to the ground on the lawn. And didn't. He was dead on the ground and also still standing. Standing on the lawn, as if nothing had happened, but you could sort of see through him and he had a faint glow about him.

He turned to me and put his left index finger to his lips. "Shhh! Don't say a word, Tommy." He turned to face the street and the departing military patrol. "Good boy, Tommy", I heard him say in my mind. Uncle Mike finished his cigarette, tossed the butt into the street, and then walked toward the sidewalk. Some sort of oval doorway appeared out of nothing. In my field, we now call that a portal. Uncle Mike, walked to the doorway. He waved to me. "See you later, Tommy." And he and the doorway vanished together.

After that, I saw ghosts. And not all ghosts are nice. And not all people are nice, either.

Dad died in 2032. That is when the army of the Illinois Apostolic Crusade was pushed out by that of the Little Egypt Righteousness Army. This bunch was more Christian Dominionist, and they didn't consider Roman Catholics or Eastern Orthodox to be Christians. I will never understand the supposed logic of how the two founding churches of Christianity are somehow not Christian, but this is the sort of shit that most of the Christian Nationalist crazies believed in. They also believe that they have the God-given right to enforce their beliefs on others, at gunpoint.

The army of the Little Egypt Christian Republic came for my sisters. Jenny was age twelve and Lexi was fourteen. As my sisters were both "Catholic heathens" the Military Authority informed us that they were taking the girls into their custody to "save their souls". They would be forcibly converted and married to military officers. My father refused and was shot dead in the front doorway. The military took Jenny and Lexi away. I never saw them again.

Grant says that Jenny was sold by the military of the Little Egypt Christian Republic to Deseret; she is still alive and a sister-wife with six children. Lexi he can find no trace of. That means that she is neither alive nor a ghost, so she is probably dead and her spirit has entered the Beyond.

Mom just disappeared the following year. She went to work at the warehouse and never came home. Other people also vanished without a trace. It had become almost "normal", not common, but not uncommon. A kind of background hum to the '30s...

We were invaded by the New Apostolic States of America in late June of 2033. They were worse than the Little Egypt Christian Republic. Under their Occupation the schools were re-opened. But, the boys and girls were separated. The girls were taught how to cook and clean, perform first aid, and religion. We boys were taught how to use a rifle, use grenades and grenade launchers, signals, and religion. Most of the religion was propaganda bullshit and unlike any form of Christianity I had ever heard of at the time or even since. It was just "batshit crazy" stuff.

And the bastards killed Grant. By then, Grant and I were eight years old. We knew little about sex and nothing about sexual orientation. But we did know abuse, and Pastor Leyton was a master in providing abuse. And he engaged in special forms of abuse with his favourites. Julian Harrison, who was eleven years old, was one of the "special favourites" of Pastor Leyton.

One afternoon, Julian was dragged into the schoolyard by the military. He was badly beaten and could barely stand. They tied him to the flagpole and called him an "abomination". They handed out rifles to us boys and we were ordered to line up, facing Julian. We were ordered to fire, on the officer's signal, at Julian. We did. We all shot him dead. Well, not all. Grant didn't. So the military took Grant away.

The next morning when we arrived at school and Grant's severely beaten body was hanging from the arch of the front gate.

I could go on, and on. The New Apostolic States of America were overrun by the Christian Reconstructionalist States of America. Then the New Apostolic States were conquered by the Christian Dominionist States. And then began the endless war, from our point of view, between the Christian Dominionists and the Christian Reconstructionalists. As our town went back and forth as territory, between these two damned theocracies. And each time, each new turnover, only brought more death.

People got by, but we were not really a town anymore. Not a community. Everyone hid. Stayed home with the doors locked and the windows boarded. They would only go out to buy food when there was no military presence on the Byway. Rise Market was open Tuesdays and Food Mart on Thursdays. I was living in an abandoned partially burnt out house on Commerce Avenue near 28th Street. The whole living room had been destroyed by fire, but the back bedrooms and kitchen were okay. I made sort of "blackout curtains" for the back part of the home, so it looked uninhabited.

Grant tells me he liked that place. It has been demolished and new homes have been built on 28th Street. They look nice.

Then there were rumours of Canadian activity up north in Carbondale and in West Frankfort. News sources were scant. Judy Chester had a ham radio, but the Christian Reconstructionalists seized that when they killed the whole Chester family. There were people in town who had rebuilt old desktop computers from spare parts. They had revived some of the old 1990s Bulletin Board Systems software, were making use active landline connections. Ava Hopkins had a node on Fidonet and when the militaries were busy fighting each other she would use it. So news of what was happening outside of town did filter in, though it would almost always be dated and the reliability questionable.

But we knew that the Canadians had liberated the Pacific Northwest from Deseret, the Texas Republic, and the Christian Dominionists. The Canadians were fighting the Christian Reconstructionalists in Ohio, and Indiana, and in northern Illinois. We also heard that the European Union, the Russian Federation, and China had requested that Canada attempt to stabilise the situation; to contain the warring successor states of the former United States of America. Canada accepted the task, and demanded support from these major powers and the United Nations, both financially and militarily, to accomplish the job. So, we were aware that the Canadians may be coming, eventually. And we hoped that they would come to Cairo.

However, nobody expected them to arrive from the south, across the Cairo Mississippi River Bridge, and coming up Highway 60.

I remember May 14, 2041. That memory is as clear now as it was a decade ago. The night of May 13 was a dangerous one. It was a night to stay in and have the lights off. And people with any sense did just that. You could hear the chaos and panic, and last minute retributions, as the Christian Reconstructionalists were pulling out. We were expecting that the army of the Christian Dominionists would be arriving soon to occupy us, once again.

So the whole town was quiet that Tuesday morning. It was cool, only about 12 degrees; sorry, 54 degrees Fahrenheit. And, it was pouring rain. I was waiting for Rise Market to open, so I could stock up on some food before it was all requisitioned by the Christian Dominionists. And that is when I saw the convoy.

Okay, it was Grant who first saw the convoy, and told me.

My first thought was, shit. Because I would not be able to purchase or trade for any food. As I watched the approaching drone swarms, I noticed that there was something off about them. They were swarms of reconnaissance drones, not attack drones. And then, squinting at the convoy vehicles, I could see that these were LUAV 7 vehicle drones followed by the LAV 8s. That was when I knew that it was the Canadians. The reconnaissance drones were now overhead and dropping leaflets. I snagged one out of the air as it drifted past me.

It was brief and stated:

'You have been LIBERATED. You are now part of the
MidWest Union, a Protectorate of Canada. Civil
administration will be restored over the next three months.
Elections are to be held next year. Legislative Assembly
of the MidWest Union'.

I didn't understand many of the words. But, I did understand that
we were now part of Canada, and that we had been liberated, and that
things were going to go back to some sort of normal. Even though the
rain was falling heavier and I was getting soaked through, I felt
something that I had not felt for a long time in my fifteen year-old life; I
felt hope.

Visual Medium Review:

For All Mankind S01 – S04
Apple TV+

I love alternate history. I love human spaceflight. Of course, I would watch a television drama that combine both. Even better, an Apollo era starting point. There was a time, back when I was age nine to twelve, when I could tell you all the acronyms used in Mission Control and their meanings, as they related to the Apollo spacecraft and spaceflight. Later on, I became more interested in the Soviet space programme, as they were still engaged in human spaceflight.

For All Mankind on Apple + hits all those checkmarks. I was going to watch this programme anyway, no matter how shitty it was. And as it was produced for Apple +, there was a very strong chance would be excellent television. It is not stated in Season 1, but the Chief Designer of the Soviet space programme, Sergei Korolev, in our timeline died in 1966 during a routine operation. As Korolev makes an appearance in Season 2, the most probable divergence point of the alternate timeline was that Korolev instead survives the surgery in 1966, which leads to the Soviets landing on the moon first. The entire series is an alternative history that plays out going forward from that point of divergence.

The race was close, and the Soviets just barely won. So, now there is competition between the superpowers and the Space Race continues on steroids.

The brilliance of this series is that the worldbuilding is solid. The showrunners have shown great research of history, the history of human spaceflight, and great attention to detail. The world feels real and possible. Almost all of the spacecraft in the series post-Apollo are based off of designs and studies that were proposed, but never built. The showrunners also don't fall into the alternate history trap of "X" change only leads to "Y" result, when "Y" can result in "AA", "AB", "AC", and even "Z" taking place. The pop culture references, even when there are alterations from our timeline, ground the world and make it more real.

The series has been criticised for being "overstuffed" with ideas and also the focus on interpersonal drama. However, I belive that both aspects have been balanced. It is best when a show can reach a wider audience. And one of the best ways to achieve that is to have a space drama that appeals to both men and women. While the average male will want the action and the tension of the accelerated and competitive space race, the average woman will want see the interpersonal dramas, especially the domestic drama arc. Then there are oddballs like me, who want to see both and done well.

The writing is spectacular. Sometimes a little slow in parts during Season 1 as the world is being built and there are characters that have to be introduced who may be minor in Season 1, and have a greater role in later seasons. And, as this is NOT a 90 minute to 2 hour movie, but ten hours of programming, there must be character depth for this to work. And character depth means more interpersonal drama (and more domestic drama). You can have cardboard characters in a movie and get away with it if there is enough action, explosions, and visual effects to drive it along to the conclusion. However, the next day, only the visual effects will be remembered by the viewer. They have seen the movie though, you want to try and lure them back for the sequel, but for television, you want to bring them back for the next episode.

The acting is superb. And the fact that the characters have depth, makes them stronger. It also gives something for actors to work with, which if the actors are of a strong calibre, and the vast majority in this cast are, tends to result in stronger performances. In addition there is solid direction and impressive visual effects.

I am offering no spoilers except for the general show premise. There are three co-creators of this series; Ronald D. Moore, Ben Nedivi, and Matt Wolpert. Moore was the showrunner for the first two seasons and Nedivi and Wolpert were the showrunners for seasons three and four. There is a different focus in the latter two seasons. Yes, the interpersonal drama plays a greater part in both latter seasons, and there are more ordinary people characters, and there are complaints that the drama overshadows the space exploration. In my opinion, this is more shift in tone. And for my tastes, I like interpersonal drama mixed in with my space exploration.

This IS one of the best science fiction shows on television today.

Neil Williams

Eight Steps

by Neil Williams

*I have a fascination for the Upper Canada Rebellion of 1937. Both
my wife and I have distant relatives who participated in that Rebellion
(on opposing sides, of course). This story has also been rewritten
multiple times, at multiple lengths, in hope of finding an audience.
Not only has it been deemed too Canadian by non-Canadians, it has
been seen that way even by Canadian fiction markets. It is also the
first of a series of stories set in this alternate history.*

The tavern room at Doel's was noisy with the sound of voices, but the unforced alto voice of Una Persson managed to part the cacophony. "...Negotiations continue between the Three Parliaments in an effort to reach an agreement to resolve the civil war. Lord Palmerston, the Crown Mediator..."

There were a few boos.

"Prime Minister Knatchbull of the Conservative Parliament..."

The boos increased in volume accompanied by some hisses.

"...assured the public that he will neither submit to Prime Minister Grey's Whig Parliament..."

The sounds of derision became scattered.

".. nor will he treat with 'the notorious rabble in Manchester'."

The boos and jeers rose in volume.

Una paused, and with smile that bore mischief, stated, "My guess is that he is referring to Prime Minister Roebuck and the Radical Parliament of the Republic of Great Britain and Ireland!"

Cheers washed back and forth through the room.

Samuel Lount took a drink from his tankard of amber ale. He was tired, very tired. It had been a tedious day in the Legislative Assembly and utterly fruitless. There was a complete deadlock. The Reformers held a minority government, but neither the Tories nor the Radicals would compromise -- on anything. Lount wasn't certain who were more to blame, Mackenzie or MacNab; both were more stubborn than any mule and neither appeared to care that the business of governing this new republic was at a standstill.

Una, perched on a high stool near a window, raised her left hand. "Quiet down, lads. You're going to want to hear this." She waited for the voices to quiet, then continued. "Knatchbull has dispatched a naval force to quell the traitorous upstarts in the Canadas, he says, 'we must endeavour to restore the rebellious Canadian colonies to the Empire and will do so by force of arms'..."

Her voice vanished, swamped with the shouts of derision.

"Greetings, friend." Joshua Doan took a seat beside him.

Hello, Josh." Lount smiled. "How do things fare in committee?"

"Alright, I guess." He took a drink of his porter. "If only Nathan Cornwall will shut his gob, we can get this damned bill to first reading." Doan sighed, "Another die-hard Family Compact minion…"

Una whistled. "How about this one, boys? From the Leeds Intelligencer on February 15, in this year of our Lord, 1836…"

There was general murmuring, but neither jeers or cheers.

Her voice had a slight Irish lilt mixed with something else that Lount could not place; maybe Polish. "The question on everybody's lips is, what happens next? This ghastly civil war is far from over. For now, there has been an end of hostilities, but this Ceasefire is tenuous. The Three Parliaments (each resolute in their claim that theirs is the one true Parliament) remain unwilling to compromise…"

"This is familiar," said Lount.

Doan nodded. "Too much so,"

Una continued reading. "…in these uncertain times, the most wise and most loyal course of action would be to take our lead from His

Majesty, who has recognized the Whig Parliament as His Parliament. With the King as our guide and faith in God, we cannot err..."

There were some muted jeers. Doel was a Reformer with Radical leanings on certain issues; the clientele at his Brewery tavern room reflected his views.

"And hear this, lads," Una projected over the din. "According to the Whig Parliament, Prime Minister Grey has stated..." There were some boos. "...the Canadas, remain part of the Empire and they have never left the Empire..." There were cheers, not rousing, but cheers. "...the only question is the true allegiance of the Canadas..." Loud boos. "...and whether their loyalty is to Great Britain..." Quiet cheers and a few jeers. "...or to the United States of America..." More boos and a few cheers from the Radicals. "Well, that says it all," Una editorialised. "Whatever we have done, or do, we are damned by both the Whigs and the Tories." Voices in agreement.

"Any movement in the Executive Council?" Doan asked.

Lount shook his head. "I am afraid, none." He took a sip of his ale. "I had a meeting, in private, with Governor Gourlay last night."

"And..."

"There are two Tories who would consider crossing the floor to the Reformers. Gourlay was wondering if any Radicals would consider doing so?" Lount paused. "He had me in mind."

"What did you tell him?"

Lount looked close into his friend's face. "I said that I would consider it. But, that I would not do it alone."

"Wise." Doan took a quick glance at the nearby tables. "The deadlock needs to be broken, else nothing can be done." He smiled. "You have my support and my trust, Sam."

"I know that, Josh." He took a deep breath. "But, do I have you? Would you also cross the floor?"

There was silence for a few moments. "That you do, Sam. Yet only if you can get two more to join us." He scanned the room. "This venture is my livelihood. I have enough trouble with MacNab and his fanatical Orangemen who threaten to burn it to the ground. I don't need to add Mackenzie's Radicals to the mix." He stood up slowly, placed a hand on Lount's shoulder and whispered in his ear, "If, and only if, Gourlay is correct about the two Tories, and you can win over two or more Radicals, then know that you have me as well." He smiled and walked away.

Una's voice continued to editorialise and read. "...And it gets more dour, my friends."

There was a scatting of boos.

"These are dark days of fear. Fear that the Republic of Great Britain and Ireland may be no more. Fear that all that had been gained at great cost -- Catholic emancipation, limited home rule for Ireland, Scotland, and Wales, and near universal suffrage by secret ballot -- has now been lost and the working people betrayed..."

Loud and jeers and boos filled the air.

"Fear that the Roebuck Ministry in Manchester has knelt before the Whig-Reformer coalition Parliament in York..."

Angry voices drowned out her voice.

#

For the third night in a row, Lount did not sleep well. It was not exactly the same dream, but similar versions of that dream haunted him. It would not leave him and deeply disturbed him. It was a nightmare dream.

His entire body shuddered and he awoke. He was sweating.

"The dream?" Una asked him. She lay there, partially sitting up, pillows propped up behind her.

"Yes," he said. He was also in a partial sitting position. "Yet, again."

Her grey eyes peered into his very being. A soft smile emerged on her fae face as she rested her chin upon her crossed arms. "Tell me what you recall."

Lount sighed. "It is all a jumble. Like last night, but also different." He paused. "Back in Britain, the Whigs and the Ultra-Tories had formed a coalition government. Although the Whigs hold the greater power, concessions had to be made to the Tories. As one of those concessions, the new government dispatched forces to the Canadas to punish the "rebellious" colonies and exact retributions. Upon their arrival, all of the Reformer and Radical members of the Assembly are arrested and tried."

"And are you?" She asked, already knowing the answer. It had been the same the previous nights.

"And I, also. If it can be called a trial. With the Canadas under martial law, these were not proper trials, merely summary military trials. We are all found guilty of high treason against the Crown. While awaiting execution at the New Gaol on Front Street, I hear that my Elizabeth was turned off our land and dispossessed by the British troops." He paused and tears flowed from his right eye. "And then, it was my day. My hands were tied behind my back, and I am lead up the eight steps to the gallows. I say some words, I don't recall what. Stupid words of hope. And I spy you in the crowd. Looking at me and calling out at me, but your words are lost within the noise of the crowd. Then the hood. The drop. And darkness."

"This is not how it ends."

"What?"

"This is not how it ends. That is what I said, Samuel." Her lips met his and they tumbled back into each other, and lustful oblivion.

Yet afterward, there is no relief. The dream returns. Again and again and again.

#

John Birnie had an excitable tenor voice. "And the Colonial Advocate states – based off of reports from the Manchester Guardian – the following. The Roebuck Ministry holds the Canadas up as, 'exemplars of colonial liberty; demonstrating that independence is not incommensurable with the Empire.' "
This was greeted with cheers.

The hatter continued. "However, the other two Parliaments do not share the same views as the Parliament of the people. While it is our profound hope that the negotiations between the Parliament of the Republic and the Whigs and Ultra-Tories bear fruit, we here in the Canadas must be wary. Who can foretell what may be visited upon us should an unholy alliance between the Whigs an Ultra-Tories emerge as the final negotiated victors of this civil war..."

Boos and raucous scorn erupted in response to these words – the Tiger Inn was another tavern frequented by Reformer and Radical supporters.

Samuel Lount sat with David Thorburn and Peter Matthews.

Matthews was uncertain. "Mac wants the Assembly to fail. It retains too much colonial baggage..."

"Rubbish!" Thornburn took a drink from his tankard. "Everyone knows that Mackenzie desires that the Canadas be annexed to the United States. We have no colonial baggage."

"And what do you call the Imperial Allegiance Act?" snapped Matthews.

"Legislation that affirms our allegiance to the British Empire as an independent, self-governing republic..."

"Allegiance and therefore colonial baggage."

"Friends," said Lount. "We are not in the Assembly; we are here to discuss options and strategy."

"Right you are, Sam," agreed Matthews. "Still, I do feel that Mac does have a point."

"And I am definite that MacNab also has a point." Lount paused. "But *are* we not here, in Toronto, to govern? And how can we do so when there is no compromise? What is for the best the republic: an Assembly crippled by deadlock and unable to pass any legislation, or a Reformer government with a weak majority?" He drank from his tankard. "I say it is the latter."

"Agreed," said Thornburn. "After all, the Republic of Lower Canada does not have this problem with their Assembly..."

"Because all of their Tories, most of the Château Clique, fled to Nova Scotia when their Assembly passed the Independence Act," retorted

Matthews.

Lount sighed. "Peter, are you so opposed to the Reformer platform, that it is impossible for you to work with them? Would it be possible for you to compromise, work with them, for the benefit of the whole Republic?"

"Can you not see..." Thornburn began.

"Hold please, David." Lount smiled. "I already know your answer. I am trying to convince Peter." Lount looked into Matthews face. "You know my convictions. They are the same as yours. The only difference is in our loyalties. In particular, our loyalty to a single man." Lount waited. "None of us are perfect. None are without flaw. I respect Mac, but my loyalty lies with our young republic. For the preservation of good government and its ability to be administered, I will betray Mackenzie and the Radicals. I will cross the floor to the Reformers."

"As will I," said Thornburn.

"And you, Peter?" asked Lount.

Matthews did not speak. His mind was in thought.

Lount waited. The silenced stretched, and then he spoke. "Can you at least ensure us that you will not reveal our plans to Mac?"

Matthews nodded slowly. The silence stretched then a slight smile crossed his lips, and Matthews sighed. "You have me, Sam. I remain a Radical, but better a Reformer government than chaos." He gave a smile. "I will cross the floor with you both."

"Aye." And Thornburn raised his tankard.

The others raised theirs as well.

"And, we hold the balance of power. They will need us to maintain their majority." Lount said with a sly grin.

#

And still he could not sleep. Or more correct, he could, but only to fall into the dream. Una's lithe body and adventurous skills in coupling could not chase the nightmare away; a nightmare that had been joined by another, equally unpleasant one.

"Describe it to me."

"This time it was not the British. It was the Americans who have invaded and conquered. The dream is less specific on how this comes to pass, only that it does so and that the Americans are unforgiving, without mercy, and inflict extreme injuries upon our inhabitants." He looked into her eyes and tried to see what she saw. Somehow she had more knowledge of these happenings than he did. "It has something to do with my plans, but somehow they go awry, and the Radicals call upon President Jackson to intervene. And that they do."

"How does it happen?"

Lount shrugged. "As before. I am found guilty of treason and sentenced to death. The execution is in stark contrast with the previous dream, as it is less orderly. In the dream, the Americans display all of the deplorable elements that Robinson, Hagerman, and MacNab consistently associate with 'republicanism'. The execution is more an example of a mob than it is judicial. The other condemned and I, our arms tied behind us, are pushed and prodded up eight steps from the cellar workshop of the millwright Morrison. I can see the calendar on a wall. It is April the twelfth. We are herded out the loading door onto an open wagon. As the nooses are tied around each of our necks, I see you in the crowd. You are trying to tell me something, but I cannot hear you. The wagon pulls away. It is a long death by strangulation, the American preferred form of hanging. I see Mac in the crowd; his gaze is fixed upon me and there is the most searing hatred in his eyes. In time, consciousness fades to darkness. And I awake, gasping for breath."

"You did." She kisses him. "This is not how it ends."

"Uh?"

"That is what I called out to you from the crowd."

"Ah, but how does it end, Una? How?"

"That will come to you."

And although sleep comes, rest does not. A third dream joins in.

When he wakes, Una asks him about it.

"It is similar to the first dream, though not the same. There has been no Civil War in the United Kingdom, there has been no independence for Upper Canada. I have risen up against the Crown and been found guilty of high treason. The time is slightly different, it is 1838. It is still April, but a different year. Peter Mathews and I are lead up out of the Gaol by an armed militia of Orangemen. We ascend the eight steps to the gallows. I say these words, 'We die in a good cause; the Canadas will yet be free.' Peter says to me, 'Sam, we lost.' And I reply, 'No; we haven't won yet.' The hoods are placed over our heads. I can feel the noose around my neck. There is a moment, and then the trap opens. I fall. Then nothing."

He touches her face. "You weren't there?"

She smiles. "Because, you are getting closer to how it is supposed to end."

He asks her to explain, but she falls silent. Then she kisses him with great passion and he is distracted in her embrace. And when they are done and nestled naked together, sleep finds them both. The nightmares come again, without pause or mercy. Over and over again. Until the three are forged together into a single, juxtaposed nightmare, which cycles throughout the seemingly endless night.

#

Lount was tired as he sat with Lewis Bright in the Sun Tavern. On his request his tankard was filled with watered-down ale.

"...Governor Gourlay was only able to convince Sandell from the Tories to cross the floor. Still, that gives you five in total – enough for a Reformer majority in the Assembly," said Bright. Bright was a young lawyer in his mid-twenties, who was the official messenger for the Governor as well as for the Legislative and Executive Councils.

"It will have to do," replied Lount. "Thank you, Lewis. Inform the Governor that I and my colleagues are ready to act."

"I will, sir." Bright stood up to leave.

"Thank you, Mr. Bright."

Lount sat there, his mind turning. The choice had been made. But was it the correct choice? Of that he remained unsure. And what of the Empire, and America...

"May, I?" The voice was a familiar one. Una Persson did not wait for an answer and sat down in the chair beside him. "Your mind appears ill at ease, Samuel." She wore her usual striped work petticoat, with a russet coloured short gown and blue check apron overtop. Her dark, lower-shoulder length hair was done in two braids that looped about her ears and peeked out from under a white muslin cap.

"You are correct, Miss Persson. If only you could quiet my thoughts."

"And what would those thoughts be?" Her grey eyes penetrated his own.

Lount, gazed into her eyes. "How does it end? You have told me how it doesn't end, but not how it shall end. What actions can I take to resolve this."

Una smiled, that smile, so lovely and so annoying. A smile that implied greater knowledge, knowledge that would not be shared. "These Canadas, you hold dear. Although they may not seem thus to you and your colleagues, or to your adversaries; they are important. They are a port of calm upon a stormy sea, a world of balance." She gave him a peck on his cheek. "You know what you will do, Sam. You have already made your decision. All that needs be done, is to act." She got up to leave. "Will I see you here later?"

Lount nodded. "You will."

Outside, the clock rang eleven.

#

It was just before the afternoon break.

Baldwin had just finished his extensive commentary regarding the Militia Reorganization bill. Speaker Robinson was about to call the vote, when Lewis Bright approached him with a message. Only my co-conspirators and I had the foreknowledge that the message was from the Governor. Robinson nodded to Bright, then spoke, "The Assembly recognizes Member Sandell."

Sandell rose from the Conservative side. "Mr. Speaker, I ask that the Assembly recognise Members Lount, Doan, Thornburn, and Matthews."

"This is most irregular," blurted MacNab.

"Member MacNab," said Robinson, "you do not have the floor. Sandell does." Robinson turned his gaze to Sandell. "Does the honourable Member request that all four men named do speak? This would be irregular."

"No, Mr. Speaker. Only that they be recognized by the Chair."

Robinson thought on this a couple of moments and then agreed. "The Assembly recognizes Member Lount, Member Doan, Member Thornburn, and Member Matthews."

The four of us rose from the Radical side. Mackenzie shot us all a dark and surprised glance, unsure as to what was afoot.

For Lount, there was the feeling that some energy, some unknown force had filled the Assembly. Lount could perceive a shimmer to the air. On either side of him, it was as if he stood within a hall of mirrors at a carnival funhouse. Lount stretched to infinity. Each image was slightly different, as was every Assembly. He had the conviction, which he could not explain, that those dreams he had been having, in some manner were actually real. And in each of the myriad reflections of himself stood Una beside him. Except for the closest reflection, that of reality. Every single Una was speaking to him.

"This, *IS* how it ends, Sam."

And in that instant Lount could perceive, yet know not how, that he was not only an active "chemical catalyst", he was also some form of anchor point. All of those nightmare realities were linked back to him, and to what he would do here today. With that realisation, he could also "see" what was like a doorway, an arch leading to new potential possibilities, that was now present and dependent upon which undertaking he was about to make.

Lount nodded to Sandell. And they both took their first step towards the Reformer side of the Assembly. That first step was the most difficult, as if he was wading in a cranberry marsh. But each step thereafter increased in ease and he felt a load lift from him. And as he walked, the mirrored images of himself seemed to collapse in number and fade. As if, they had existed as some potential reality and that his actions had now turned them into mere phantoms. And for a moment, he had a

35

glimpse of the potential realities that his steps were manifesting into existence, and those were good –- for him and for the Canadas.

It was eight steps to cross the floor, perhaps more for the others, as he does have a tall frame. Lount reached out and shook Sandell's hand. Then the five of us shook hands, before being welcomed by our, now, fellow Reformers. He looked back across the floor and met Mackenzie's gaze. He was seething with quiet rage. MacNab was also unfriendly in his countenance, but he did nod to Lount – accepting a play well made.

#

The clock had just struck seven. There was a large crowd in the Sun Tavern. Musicians would be playing in half an hour. The mood is raucous, some because of Reformer majority government, most in anticipation of the music and the dancing.

Lount sat on the bench of one of the long tables. Una sat next to him, his left arm around her waist. Matthews and Thornburn had just left for Doan's Brewery, to check the mood among the Radicals. Lount knew that it would be wise for him to stay away from Doan's for at least a few days, and from the Tiger for a few weeks. He shrugged inwardly. His thoughts were still focused on the Legislature and the work ahead.

Una pinched him. "Samuel Lount. It is time to leave the Assembly for tonight. Are there not better things to think upon?"

His gaze shifted to the young woman next to him and with that his thoughts did also. "And what should I be thinking on?"

"Perhaps, what we should do together this evening." Her eyes held a deep smouldering sensuality.

"Ah yes, the dancing."

"And later?"

"Yes, later. That has not been determined."

"Really. I was certain that it had already been decided."

"Miss Persson, I fear for damage to your reputation."

She laughed. "You fear for the reputation of a barmaid and sometimes newsreader? You are truly a wonder, Samuel Lount." And with that she kissed him.

There was a commotion by the bar. Lewis Bright yelling something, excited and happy, to Elliott, the owner of the Sun.

Elliott jumped up onto the bar and shouted. "Persson! Una, are you still here?"

"Yes." Una stood up. "What is it you want?"

"Come over here and read this to everyone. It just came in from England."

Una disengaged from Lount and made her way over to the bar, the crowd making way for her. Elliott and Bright helped pull her up onto the bar. Elliot handed her the broadsheet.

Una gave the page a glance over and a huge smile crept onto her lips. "Quiet everybody!" She waited for the noise to subside. "His Majesty, William IV, King of the United Kingdom of Great Britain and Ireland does announce that both the Radical Parliament of Manchester and the Conservative Parliament of Westminster have dissolved and accept that the Whig Parliament in York is the true Parliament. The Parliament shall be restored to Westminster immediately, as will the machineries of government. The British Civil War has ended..."

There were cheers.

"... the three Parliaments agreed on the following terms: dissolution of the Conservative and Radical Parliaments. Restoration of the Whig Parliament as His majesty's government in Westminster. Silence! Hear this." She paused. "Catholic emancipation, universal suffrage by secret ballot, one third of the House of Lords to be merit peers, limited home rule for Ireland, Scotland, and Wales..."

There were happy shouts and cheers.

"Recognition of the Canadas as independent republics within the British Empire..."

If there were anything else it was drowned out by the joyous noise of the crowd. Una started to continue, but there was no point. The crowd was too loud. She shrugged and handed the broadsheet back to Bright. Lount had already made his way over to where she stood on the bar. Una jumped down into his arms. Everyone was happy. Elliot signalled for the musicians to start now. And the dancing began.

#

Much later that night, Samuel Lount held Una spooned close to him in bed. And that night sleep did find him. And if he did have any dreams at all, he recalled them not.

CLOSING PAGES

Neil Williams

When is the use of another author's character an act of plagiarism or just making use of an "open-source character"? This is a good question; though my answer, demonstrated in "Eight Steps", is obviously clear.

I never read the science fiction juveniles. I began with the adult science fiction of Arthur C. Clarke and branched out from there. I had a friend who was into the New Wave and was exposed to Michael Moorcock. I read the first three Cornelius books at too young an age to have a true appreciation for them. Similar for the works of Ballard, and Malzberg, and Ellison, and Spinrad. Many of the nuances were lost on me. I still read them, but also began to shift away from books that were difficult reads, and that I felt (correctly), that I was missing a lot from. I would return to these works in my mid-twenties, but for the rest of my teens, I dove into space opera. Though I did read some other Moorcock novels, including "Warlord of the Air" and "The Land Leviathan".

Of the characters that I was first introduced to in the Cornelius books, I found Una Persson the most interesting. Even more so, when she also appeared in the Oswald Bastable novels. I would say that in some ways Una Persson was an idealised fantasy woman for me, a kind of manic pixie anarchist revolutionary dream girl. However, my recent re-read of Hillary Bailey's "Everything Blowing Up: An Adventure of Una Persson", does make me wonder if Moorcock felt the same way towards this character (or at the least that his first wife, alludes in subtext that she felt that she had "competition" from this fictional woman).

So, I had an interest in Una Persson. But as I reached my mid twenties and beyond, that allure was tarnished by critique. Persson is also a flawed character with sharp dichotomies. A juxtaposition between having an actually achievable goal and the chic nihilism of wanton destruction. Still, it was Una who was my first exposure to anarchist political thought.

This political stanch would also be tempered and challenged by my girlfriends during this time period, who did try their best to make me see the horrid error of my ways, and thus see the light of the one, true, pure form of socialism (be that Moscow line, Maoist line, Albanian line, Romanian line, and so on...). But, all of these true and pure paths were flawed, and foreign. I had already come to the realisation that one size does not fit all.

Thus, I have worn my Marxist stamped label as a badge of honour; I remain a "petty bourgeois anarchist revolutionist". Yet, I am a person who has worked in blue collar, who does have a great understanding of all of the parts that go into producing our finished goods that we use and depend upon, and that it is a lot easier to destroy than to build, and that building is the better approach (which lacks any immediate gratification) and that takes much longer. And that any real socialist movement has to be grounded within the history and the culture of the people building it (any foreign imports have to be extensively modified to fit the society they have been imported into).

Thus, like Una, I have an individualist anarchist side that says fuck the system and to hell with copyright. Simultaneously, I also don't want to give the capitalist elites anything for free (be that my fiction, my course development, or my textbooks), that they can and will profit from and exploit. If everyone is doing open source, even the major creative conglomerates; sure, I am all in.

Michael Moorcock has stated and re-stated numerous times that the characters of the Jerry Cornelius universe, in particular Jerry Cornelius, were a kind of shared fictional universe, that writers could play with these "toys" in a sort-of precursor to "open source". Of course, it is considered polite to first ask to play with Michael's "toys", and to treat those "toys" with respect while playing with them. I asked to play with one "toy" well over a year ago. I did request a second time, but I believe my request failed to make it past the "gatekeepers". As my requests were neither denied, just ignored; I am taking for granted that what was once upon a time stated back in the 1970s, and reaffirmed in 2003 and 2007, still stands in the present, and that permission is not required.

I believe that those who have read "Eight Steps" can confirm that I treated the character of Una Persson with respect. After all, I have long had an affinity for this woman and like Michael Moorcock himself, have often wished she would visit me sometime. Of course, that carries a degree of danger. Where Una goes, in most parts of the multiverse, she brings a shit storm with her...

"Eight Steps" is the first story in Bastards of the Empire, a series of short fiction that does follow the Lount family and their descendants. Una Persson, as a temporal adventuress, is a bridge across the decades; someone who is ageless and also has intimate knowledge of what previously occurred. She also makes "guest appearances" in the "Ministry of If" series, that secret agency of the Canadian government that seeks to preserve the timeline from interference.

In closing, I hope that you have enjoyed this 50th Anniversary edition of Sirius Science Fiction. See you next fall...

CODA

SWILL is the science fiction op-ed publication of the Uldune Media imprint Vile Fen Press. SWILL has been published inconstantly since 1981.

A current list of SWILL volumes:

Original SWILL	issues 1 through 7
SWILL 2011	issues 8 through 12
SWILL 2012	issues 13 through 17
SWILL 2013	issues 18 through 22
SWILL 2014	issues 23 through 26
SWILL 2015	issues 27 through 30

Vile Fen Press
a division of Klatha Entertainment an Uldune Media company